Piddle Diddle's Lost Hat

Written by Wayne A. Major
and Co-Author Ralphine Major

Illustrated by Teresa Wilkerson

Piddle Diddle's Lost Hat

Written by Wayne A. Major and Co-Author Ralphine Major
Illustrated by Teresa Wilkerson
Book design by Tara Sizemore
Published June 2015
Little Creek Books
Imprint of Jan-Carol Publishing, Inc

You may contact the publisher:
Jan-Carol Publishing, Inc
PO Box 701
Johnson City, TN 37605
publisher@jancarolpublishing.com
jancarolpublishing.com

Dedicated in memory of our father,
Ralph O. Major, who passed away in 1994.
He instilled in us a love for animals;
and
in honor of our mother, Juanita D. Major,
who has worked tirelessly alongside us to bring
Piddle Diddle into the homes of children.

" . . . Blessed rather are those who hear the word of God and obey it."
Luke 11:28 (NIV)

"IT'S SNOWING!"
exclaimed Piddle Diddle,
her eyes wide with excitement.

PETEY'S ROOM
Hockey Jr.

She shouted to her big brother. "PETEY, WAKE UP!
Let's go outside and have a snowball fight,"
Piddle Diddle begged.

Petey put on his bright blue hat and pulled the flaps down over his ears. Piddle Diddle wrapped a bright yellow scarf around her neck and put her pink pocketbook with her P. D. initials on her flipper.

She reached for her hat, but it was gone!
"Petey, have you seen my hat?" Piddle Diddle asked.

"No," Petey answered. "Let's go look for it."

They grabbed their snowboards and headed
to the ocean, but they could not find
Piddle Diddle's hat anywhere.
"WHERE COULD IT BE?"
Piddle Diddle screamed loudly.

PD

"Where could what be?" came a voice from behind them. It was their friend, Pandi, the polar bear cub.

"I lost my Santa Claus hat," Piddle Diddle said. "Have you seen it?"

"No, Piddle Diddle," Pandi answered. "I have been fishing all day, but I have not seen your hat. I do hope you find it."

Piddle Diddle was sad because
she could not find her hat.

Suddenly, Petey and Piddle Diddle heard a loud noise.
SWISH! SWISH! SWISH!
A big pile of snow fell all around them.
Then, they saw Artie, the arctic fox.

"Hello, Petey. Hello, Piddle Diddle.
What brings you out this way?" Artie asked.

"We're looking for Piddle Diddle's hat." Petey answered.

"Hat? What kind of hat?" Artie asked in a sharp voice.

"It's my red Santa Claus hat with a white
fuzzy ball on the end." Piddle Diddle said.
"And it's my favorite one!"

Artie thought for a moment as he swished his bushy tail.
"I have not seen a red Santa Claus hat," Artie said.
"But, I will look for it on my way home. You need to
find your hat, because it is very cold out here."
Artie gave his bushy tail another swish.
"Oh my goodness!" he exclaimed.
"I must be on my way. It's time for lunch!"
Then he scampered out of sight.

Piddle Diddle and Petey sat down by a big pile
of rocks to rest. "Where could it be?"
Piddle Diddle sighed as she looked up toward the sky.

"PETEY, LOOK!" Piddle Diddle yelled.
"I see my hat on top of the rocks!"
Piddle Diddle made a snowball and threw
it as hard as she could up on the big pile of rocks.
BAM!
The snowball smashed into a million snowflakes
and fell all over Piddle Diddle!
But, her hat was still on the rocks.

PD

Petey started climbing up the rock pile and fell
back down. Piddle Diddle started climbing
up the rocks but could not reach her hat.

"HOOT, HOOT. What are you doing?" asked a voice.
Petey and Piddle Diddle turned to see their friend,
Sparky, the white snowy owl.

"We are trying to get Piddle Diddle's hat off of the rocks,"
Petey answered. "Can you help us?"

Sparky flapped his big wings and soared up to the top
of the rock pile. He plucked the hat from the rocks
and SWOOSHED back down.

Piddle Diddle was so excited! She jumped up and down and clapped her flippers.

"Oh, thank you, Sparky," she said as he handed her the Santa Claus hat. Piddle Diddle was so happy to finally get her lost hat. She put it on and tossed her head.

Petey and Piddle Diddle got on their snowboards
and started down the hill toward home.
"WHEE!"
Piddle Diddle exclaimed. She laughed as the white
fuzzy ball hit her in the face.

"Where did you find your hat?"
their mother asked when they got home.

Piddle Diddle proudly said, "When I have a problem
I cannot solve myself, I always remember to ask
my friends for help." Then, she told how Sparky
helped get her hat off of the rocks.

Petey warmed in front of a roaring fire as Piddle Diddle took off her hat. "I am so happy because I found my FAVORITE hat!" she said.

Piddle Diddle's mother chuckled as she put
Piddle Diddle to bed. She wondered if Piddle Diddle
goes looking for trouble or if trouble comes looking
for Piddle Diddle. Either way, Piddle Diddle
was already fast asleep, dreaming about the fun
she would have tomorrow.

Wayne Major

During the years Wayne and his sister, Ralphine Major, helped teach kindergarten classes at church, he admired the children's eagerness and willingness to learn. Wayne created the character, Piddle Diddle, the Widdle Penguin. He grew up on a dairy farm and has always enjoyed being around animals and reading about them. Wayne is an Old West history buff, and all of the cowboy actors were his heroes. He is a new hobbyist in "O" gauge model trains and wants to build a layout of the Old West. A resident of Corryton in rural East Tennessee, Wayne majored in Marketing at The University of Tennessee and graduated with a Business Administration degree. He is employed by the State of Tennessee and credits Ralphine with coordinating many of the business contacts for this book. Through this book they have seen God work and realize how important it is to wait on God's timing.

Ralphine Major

Ralphine is thrilled to join Wayne in writing books for children. She has a Business Administration degree from The University of Tennessee with a major in Office Administration and minor in Education and enjoys watching the Tennessee VOLS in basketball and football and the Lady VOLS in basketball. She is retired from the Tennessee Valley Authority (TVA). Though she has never had a journalism class, Ralphine uses her God-given talent as a contributing writer of true, human-interest stories for *The Knoxville Focus* (www.knoxfocus.com). She grew up on the same dairy farm as Wayne and still resides in Corryton.

Read more at majorbooksofjoy.com

Teresa Wilkerson

Teresa was born, raised and still resides in Greene County in a beautiful area of Eastern Tennessee. She grew up on the dairy farm that her family still runs today. Teresa has worn several hats in her lifetime from daughter and farm girl to wife and mother, business partner, widow, grandmother and artist. Art, in some form or fashion, has been a big part of Teresa's life. She has worked in the area of portraiture, both of people and that of pets, mural work for schools and churches, along with various other artistic pursuits. At this point in life, though, she is putting a very concentrated effort in the area of illustration, specifically, children's book illustration.